Too Many Hopkins

Written and illustrated by

Tomie dePaola

G.P. Putnam's Sons
New York

"Well," said Daddy Hopkins, looking out at the fine spring morning. "It's time to plant our gardens."

"This year, Daddy and I want all of you children to help," said Mommy Hopkins.

"Oh, goody!" cried the fifteen little Hopkins.

Mr. and Mrs. Hopkins had the finest and most beautiful vegetable and flower gardens in all of Fiddle-Dee-Dee Farms.

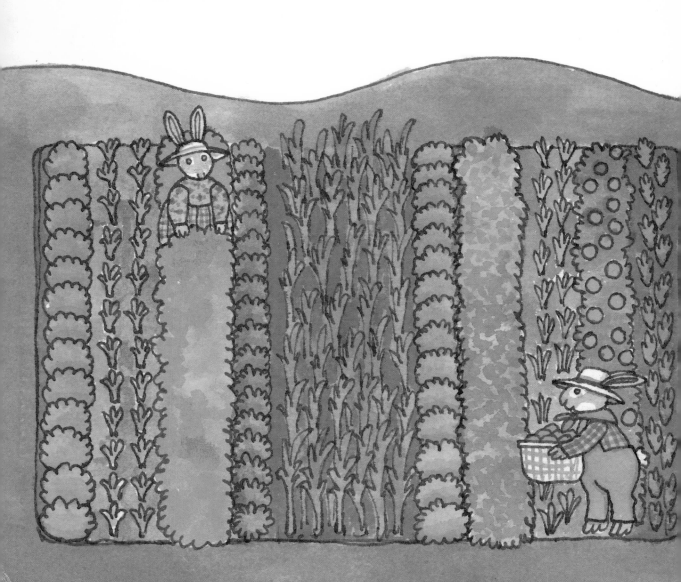

Every spring, they would dig up the earth and rake it smooth. Next they would make long straight rows and put in the seeds. Finally they would cover the seeds and water them.

"When can we begin?" shouted the Hopkins children.

"This morning," said Daddy Hopkins. "While Mommy and I go to the store to buy carrot seeds, you can all start on the small radish garden. Now, line up so I can tell you what to do."

"Willy, Wiley, Wally, Wendy and Winny, take the spades and start digging up the earth."

"Hurrah!" cried the quintuplets.

"Bunny, Bonny, Billy and Biff, you four can rake," said Mommy Hopkins.

"Hooray," cried the quadruplets.

"Flossie, Frannie and Fuffie, you make the rows for the seeds," said Daddy.

"Goody!" cried the triplets.

"Skipper and Skeezer," said Mommy, "you..."

"We know, we know. Plant the seeds," cried the twins.

"And what do I do?" asked Petey.

"You get to water it!" the Hopkins all shouted.

"Now, everyone to work," said Mommy and Daddy.

The Hopkins children ran to the garden. They could almost taste the fat pink radishes. They started in—all at the same time.

"We're supposed to dig first," said Willy, Wiley, Wally, Wendy and Winny.

"Wait until we rake," said Bunny, Bonny, Billy and Biff.

"Don't plant those seeds yet!" shouted Flossie,
Frannie and Fuffie.

"You're getting us all wet," cried Skipper and
Skeezer.

"It's my JOB," said Petey.

"What a mess!" cried Daddy Hopkins, home from the store. "There are too many Hopkins!"

"Now, now," said Mommy. "Let's start again. Everyone sit down."

"All right, quintuplets—DIG—"
Willy, Wiley, Wally, Wendy and Winny dug.

"Next—quadruplets—rake."
Bunny, Bonny, Billy and Biff raked.

"Triplets—make the rows."
Flossie, Frannie and Fuffie made the rows.

"Twins—plant the seeds."
Skipper and Skeezer planted the seeds.

"Petey—turn on the hose!" Petey did. And the radish garden was ready to grow.

"You see," said Mommy Hopkins. "There are not too many Hopkins."

"You're right," said Daddy Hopkins. "There are not too many Hopkins when they are not all in the same place at the same time."